D1148755

0129520345

FERGUS in the PARK

Dedicated to
Cannon Hill Park, Birmingham,
where as a child I enjoyed
many happy family outings.

First published in Great Britain in 2006
by Piccadilly Press Ltd,
5 Castle Road, London NW1 8PR
www.piccadillypress.co.uk

Text and illustrations copyright © Tony Maddox, 2006

All rights reserved. No part of this publication may be reproduced,
stored in a retrieval system, or transmitted, in any form or by any
means, electronic, mechanical, photocopying or otherwise, without
prior permission of the copyright owner.

The right of Tony Maddox to be recognised as Author and
Illustrator of this work has been asserted by him in accordance
with the Copyright, Designs and Patents Act 1988.

Designed by Tony Maddox and Simon Davis

Printed and bound in China by WKT
Colour reproduction by Dot Gradations Ltd, UK

ISBN: 1 85340 854 9 (hardback)
EAN: 9 781853 408540
1 85340 859 X (paperback)
EAN: 9 781853 408595

1 3 5 7 9 10 8 6 4 2

A catalogue record of this book is available from the British Library

FERGUS in the PARK

Tony Maddox

WARWICKSHIRE LIBRARY
& INFORMATION SERVICE

012952034 5

£5.99	24-Nov-06
PB	-5 JAN 2007
pinman	

Piccadilly • London

Fergus was waiting in
the truck for Farmer Bob.
It was a warm, sunny day.

He could see the park across the street.
It looked cool and inviting.

He knew he should
stay in the truck, but the
park was too tempting.
He jumped down and
went to take a look.

"This is better than sitting in the back of Farmer Bob's old truck," he thought, as he strolled through the trees.

He stopped to watch the skateboarders
zooming up and down.

He began to imagine that he was a champion skateboarder, performing all sorts of tricks. Wouldn't that be fun?

His daydreams were broken by
an angry shout behind him.

He turned to see the park keeper
hurrying towards him.

"Can't you read?" he demanded,
pointing to a large sign.
Fergus was puzzled.
"What a silly question," he thought.
"Of course I can't read. I'm a dog!"

In this situation, the best thing to do was ...

RUN!

Through the park he raced, with the park keeper close behind. Other dogs, excited by all the commotion, broke loose from their owners and joined in the chase.

The park keeper was getting closer and closer.
"He's going to catch me!" groaned Fergus.

When he saw the
skateboard lying at
the edge of the path,
he jumped on it,
and off he went!

People scattered as he whizzed along.

He was going *FASTER*…

and *FASTER*…

and *FASTER*.

The boating lake was just ahead…

Boats
for
HIRE

HOW WAS HE GOING TO STOP?

Too late! There he was…
flying UP…UP…UP into the air…
and then *down…down …down*

into the lake with a great *BIG SPLASH!*

He began to swim towards the
island in the middle of the lake.
"I'll be safe there," he gasped.

But he wasn't...
The park keeper was
climbing into a rowing boat.
He was coming out to the island!
"This is turning into a really bad day!"
sighed Fergus, miserably.

But help was at hand.
The ducks who lived on the island
thought of a way Fergus could escape
without the park keeper knowing.

Together, with Fergus hidden in the middle,
they paddled slowly past the park keeper
and back to the park.

As Fergus hurried back to Farmer Bob's truck, the ducks kept the park keeper busy by surrounding his boat, flapping their wings and making lots of noise.

"Sorry I've taken so long, Fergus,"
said Farmer Bob when he returned.

"I know! As you've been so good,
we'll go for a walk in the park!"